Welcome to an exciting world of hilarious questions about the eating habits of animals. Just in case some of them seem unfamiliar ...

The **durian**, a popular fruit in Southeast Asia, is about the size and shape of a soccer ball but is covered in hard, short yellowish green spikes. The yellow flesh inside is soft like custard and tastes creamy and sweet. Durians have such a strong smell that some people won't go near them! **Cantaloupes** are also about the size of a soccer ball, with yellowish orange flesh and a sweet taste. American cantaloupes have khaki-colored, rough-netted skin with green undertones. Another tropical fruit, a **rambutan,** looks like a bright red golf ball covered with whiskery hairs. Inside, the flesh is white, sweet and juicy, and covers a seed you can't eat. **Prunes** are sweet dried plums, dark in color and wrinkled. They are good for your health and digestion, but if you eat too many, you might end up in the bathroom! **Figs,** native to the Mediterranean region, are soft and sweet, full of tiny seeds, and are often eaten dried.

Possums, a diverse group of mammals, are found in Australia, and North and South America. American possums (like the ones in this book) have no hair on their tails. Some say they look like overgrown rats! But to an Australian, possums have bushy tails. **Grunions** are small fish, about 5 to 6 inches in length, with bluish green backs, and silvery sides and bellies. They are native to the shores of southern California and are the only fish to lay eggs on sandy beaches. **Raccoons** are found on a few tropical islands, and in North and South America. They will eat almost anything. They are small, with a black vertical mark on their forehead, black rings around their eyes with white fur above the black rings, and a bushy black-ringed tail. **Mink** are weasel-like, about the size of a house cat, and dark chocolate brown in color. In some countries they are raised on farms and their fur is used to make expensive mink coats, but many people frown on this. **Gnats** are tiny flying insects that bite people and usually live near water. **Puffins** are black and white sea-birds with large brightly-colored beaks. **Yetis** are large hairy humanoid creatures said to roam high in the Himalayan Mountains in Tibet. Some say they are real but no one has ever seen one!

Published by Tuttle Publishing,
an imprint of Periplus Editions (HK) Ltd,
with editorial offices at 153 Milk Street,
Boston, Massachusetts 02109 and 130 Joo
Seng Road #06-01, Singapore 368357.

Text © 2005 Periplus Editions (HK) Ltd
Illustrations © 2005 Roger Clarke
For Bo Jun, thanks for your support
and belief in me.—*Roger Clarke*

LCC Card No: 2004110837
ISBN 0-8048-3643-4
First printing, 2005
Printed in Singapore
08 07 06 05 04
6 5 4 3 2 1

Distributed by:
North America, Latin America & Europe
Tuttle Publishing, 364 Innovation Drive
North Clarendon, VT 05759-9436, USA
tel: (802) 773 8930, fax: (802) 773 6993
email: info@tuttlepublishing.com
website: www.tuttlepublishing.com

Asia Pacific
Berkeley Books Pte Ltd
130 Joo Seng Road #06-01
Singapore 368357
tel: (65) 6280 1330, fax: (65) 6280 6290
email: inquiries@periplus.com.sg
website: www.periplus.com

Japan
Tuttle Publishing
Yaekari Building, 3F
5-4-12 Osaki, Shinagawa-ku
Tokyo 141-0032
tel: (03) 5437 0171, fax: (03) 5437 0755
email: tuttle-sales@gol.com

Do Mice Eat Rice?

Did you ever wonder
why we eat what we do?

TUTTLE PUBLISHING
Boston • Rutland, Vermont • Tokyo

And why we turn up our nose at something new?
Why some people like what others don't?
Why some people eat what others won't?

Do you think that's true of other creatures too?

Do you suppose that bears would eat pears?

I'll bet they would if they could.
Pears are good.

I know for a fact that mice eat rice.
I've seen them, twice.

I'm also quite sure that bats eat gnats.
And if they could, cats would eat rats.
But then again, some rats might eat cats.

I have heard that goats eat oats,
but if you don't watch them,
they'll also eat coats,
and shirts and skirts,
and ties and pies,
and newspapers and books and ...

But wouldn't it be silly if a billy ate a chili?

Do you suppose that parrots
would eat carrots?
Or bees would eat cheese?
Would lizards eat gizzards?
Or dogs eat frogs?

Most poodles would eat oodles of noodles, I'll bet.

Do you think apes would eat grapes?

Or snakes would eat cakes?

Would possums eat blossoms?

And raccoons eat prunes?

Have you ever seen antelope eat cantaloupe?
Or stallions eat scallions?
Or puffins eat muffins?

I'll bet no one has seen a yeti named Betty eating spaghetti!

Without a doubt, pigs would eat figs,
and it wouldn't surprise me
if they even ate twigs.
But I am certain pigs don't like onions,
although they might eat grunions.

Do you think a mink
would drink ink?

Or a bee would drink tea?

Or drakes would
drink shakes?

Do you suppose a moth
would drink broth?

I really doubt that a moose would drink juice,

but I'll bet an otter would drink water.

If he didn't, he ought'er.

I can't imagine that a ram would eat jam?
But it might eat a yam?
I'm quite sure it wouldn't eat ham.

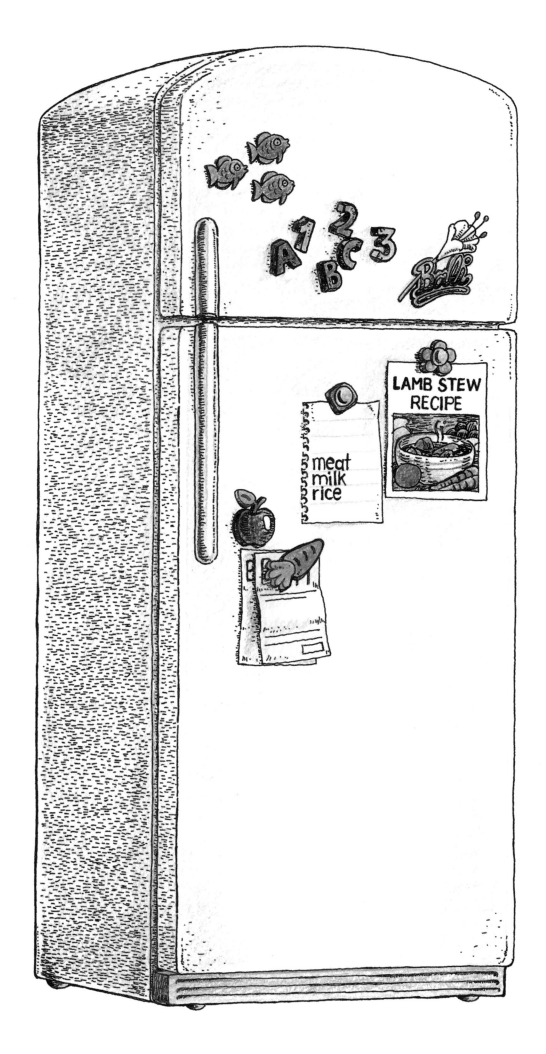

And I really doubt that a ewe would eat stew.
But who knows? Do you?

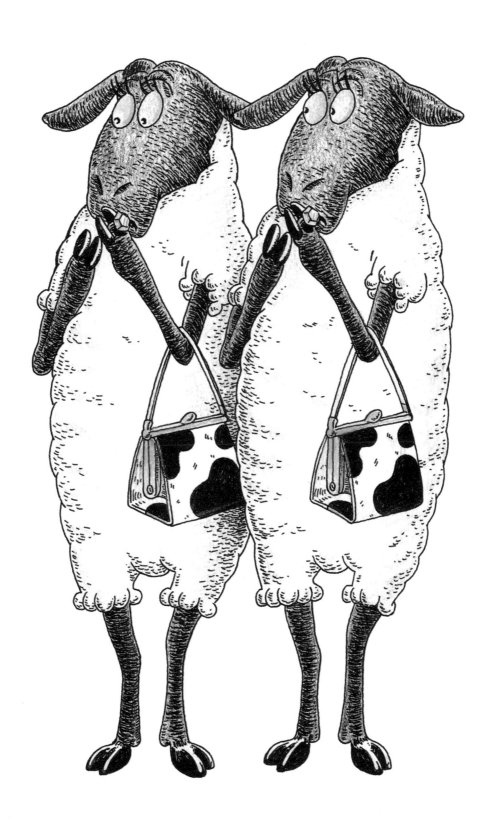

I am sure of this, at least,
every beast enjoys its own feast.

I do too. Don't you?